# Sight Word Tales™

this is too for

# A House for Mouse

by Maria Fleming
illustrated by Tammie Lyon

## SCHOLASTIC INC.

New York • Toronto • London • Auckland • Sydney
Mexico City • New Delhi • Hong Kong • Buenos Aires

Designed by Maria Lilja
ISBN-13: 978-0-545-01646-9 • ISBN-10: 0-545-01646-0
Copyright © 2007 by Scholastic Inc.
All rights reserved. Printed in China.

First printing, October 2007

12 11 10 9 8 7 6 5 4 3 2 1    7 8 9 10 11 12/0

**Too** big!

Mouse needs a house.
**This** house **is too** big **for** Mouse.

**This** house **is too** small.

**This** house **is too** round **for** Mouse.

**This** house **is too** tall.

**This** house **is too** loud **for** Mouse.

**This** house **is too** hairy.

This house **is too** hot **for** Mouse.

**This** house **is too** scary.

This house **is too** cold **for** Mouse.

**This** house **is too** bright.

**This** house **is too** wet **for** Mouse.

**This** house **is** just right!

# Sight Word Review

Do you know the four sight words in this book? Read aloud the word on each brick.

this

too    for    is

for    too

is    this

14

# Sight Word Fill-ins

this    is
too    for

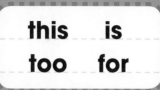

Listen to the sentences. Then choose a sight word from the box to fill in each blank.

**Word Box**   **this**       **is**          **too**        **for**

1   We had pizza ___For___ lunch.

2   My mom made me ___a___ hat.

3   I was ___too___ sick to go.

4   These books are ___for___ you.

5   My favorite snack ___is___ popcorn.

6   What is ___The___ mouse doing in my room?

7   He ___was___ my friend.

8   It was ___To___ cold to swim.

# Sight Word Cheers

**Celebrate the four new sight words you learned by saying these short cheers.**

**T-h-i-s!** Give a yell!
What do these four letters spell?
A sight word that we all know well —
**This, this, this!**

**I-s!** Give a yell!
What do these two letters spell?
A sight word that we all know well —
**Is, is, is!**

**T-o-o!** Give a yell!
What do these three letters spell?
A sight word that we all know well —
**Too, too, too!**

**F-o-r!** Give a yell!
What do these three letters spell?
A sight word that we all know well —
**For, for, for!**